P9-DNM-495
3 5674 03594995 8

ADDY STUDIES FREEDOM

BY CONNIE PORTER

ILLUSTRATIONS DAHL TAYLOR

VIGNETTES RENÉE GRAEF, PHILIP HOOD, JANE VARDA

THE AMERICAN GIRLS COLLECTION®

Published by Pleasant Company Publications

For information, address: Book Editor, Pleasant Company Publications, 8400 Fairway Place, P.O. Box 620998, Middleton, WI 53562.

Visit our Web site at **americangirl.com**

Printed in Singapore.
02 03 04 05 06 07 08 09 TWP 10 9 8 7 6 5 4 3 2 1

Library of Congress Cataloging-in-Publication Data

Porter, Connie Rose, 1959–
Addy studies freedom / by Connie Porter ;
illustrations, Dahl Taylor ; vignettes, Renée Graef, Philip Hood, Jane Varda.
p. cm. — (The American girls collection)
Summary: Addy's jubilation over her family's new freedoms
is cut short by the news that President Lincoln has been shot and killed.

ISBN 1-58485-480-4
1. African Americans—Juvenile fiction. 2. Lincoln, Abraham, 1809–1865—Assassination—Juvenile fiction. [1. African Americans—Fiction. 2. Lincoln, Abraham, 1809–1865—Assassination—Fiction] I. Taylor, Dahl, ill. II. Graef, Renée, ill. III. Hood, Philip, ill. IV. Varda, Jane, ill. V. Title. VI. Series.
PZ7.P825 Ade 2002 [Fic]—dc21 2001036376

OTHER AMERICAN GIRLS SHORT STORIES:

FELICITY DISCOVERS A SECRET

JUST JOSEFINA

KIRSTEN AND THE CHIPPEWA

SAMANTHA'S BLUE BICYCLE

KIT'S HOME RUN

MOLLY'S A+ PARTNER

Picture Credits

The following individuals and organizations have generously given permission to reprint illustrations contained in "Looking Back": p. 38—Artist, Francis Bicknell Carpenter; p. 39—Playbill, Harvard Theatre Collection, Harvard University; Gun, NPS, Ford's Theatre, Washington, DC, photographed by Edward Owen; p. 40—Sermon flyer, Eugene Boss Collection, Georgetown University Library, Special Collections Division, Washington, DC; Train, Courtesy of the Illinois State Historical Library; p. 42—(detail) W146,7929.F, The Library Company of Philadelphia; p. 44—Courtesy Meserve-Kunhardt Collection, Mt. Kisco, NY; p. 45—National Archives and Records Administration; p. 46—© Medford Historical Society Collection/CORBIS; p. 47—Mourning card, Eugene Boss Collection, Georgetown University Library, Special Collections Division, Washington, DC; Mourning badge, Courtesy Meserve-Kunhardt Collection, Mt. Kisco, NY; p. 48—Photography by Jamie Young.

Table of Contents

POPPA
Addy's father, whose dream gives the family strength.

MOMMA
Addy's mother, whose love helps the family survive.

ADDY
A courageous girl, smart and strong, growing up during the Civil War.

SAM
Addy's sixteen-year-old brother, determined to be free.

ESTHER
Addy's two-year-old sister.

M'DEAR
An elderly woman who befriends Addy.

MISS DUNN
Addy's kind and patient teacher, who doesn't like lines to be drawn between people.

SARAH MOORE
Addy's good friend.

MR. AND MRS. GOLDEN
The owners of the boarding house where the Walkers live.

ADDY STUDIES FREEDOM

One Friday afternoon as Addy and her friend Sarah came skipping out of the Sixth Street School, Addy was bursting with good news. She'd held it in all day, and now she let it spill out. "My Poppa going south on a train to get Esther, Sam, Auntie Lula, and Uncle Solomon. It's like the best dream in the world!"

The Sunday before, the Civil War had ended. Addy, Momma, and Poppa had celebrated at a citywide party that lasted all night. It had been better than a dream, because when Addy woke the next morning, what had happened was real. President Lincoln had ended slavery and brought the country back together. Now it was safe for Poppa to go back south.

Sarah skipped faster, her school sack flapping at her side as she tried to keep up with Addy. "Maybe you could write about it for the theme Miss Dunn give us," Sarah said.

Miss Dunn had given the class an assignment to write a one-page theme over the weekend called "Why My Heart Is Glad My Country Is Free." Miss Dunn got the idea from a slogan printed on banners carried through the city the night the war ended. The teacher said each student was to write about what freedom meant to him or her.

"That's a good idea. If my Poppa had tried to go just last week, he could've been put back into slavery," Addy said. "This week, he free to go wherever he want."

"Except eat inside a ice cream parlor right here in Philadelphia," said Sarah.

"Or ride inside a streetcar," Addy added. She turned around and waited with Sarah on the curb as two streetcars came barreling down the street.

As Addy and Sarah waited for

them to pass, Addy heard two black men talking. They were near the curb, shoveling manure from the street into a cart.

The younger one said, "You'll see now that the war over. There gonna be so much money around, it's gonna start piling up in the streets."

"Is that right?" asked the older man, emptying his shovel into the cart.

"Sure is. We gonna need shovels bigger than these to scoop it up."

The men stopped and looked up at Addy and Sarah.

"Don't pay this man no mind, young ladies," the older man said. "He crazy."

"Oh, no, I'm not crazy. Girls, get your

shovels ready," said the younger man.

Addy and Sarah laughed as the men moved on. When they stepped up onto the curb on the other side of the street, Addy saw a shiny penny on the mucky sidewalk.

Picking up the penny, Addy said, "Maybe that man was right."

When Sarah turned to go home, Addy walked on, noticing the people around her in the crowded streets. They all seemed happy—black and white people, old and young people. Many smiled, greeting one another as they passed. It even looked to Addy as if the horses were pausing to greet each other with whinnies. *Maybe,* Addy thought, *they studying on freedom too now that the war over.*

It seemed to Addy that she had been studying on freedom forever, thinking, wondering, worrying about it. There was so much she wanted to write in her paper, but words didn't come easily to her. They were inside her head, so right and clear, but when she tried to put them on paper, they were cloudy as water just drawn from a well. Addy wanted her words about freedom to be just right.

Before supper, Addy sat cross-legged on the floor beside her bed, letting the words trickle out.

For me if my heart had wings it would fly up the sky and everybody would see me

Before supper, Addy sat cross-legged on the floor beside her bed, letting the words trickle out.

flying over top the moon like that cow jumping over the moon. My heart glad there no more slavery. My sister and brother free. My aunt and uncle free. Every slave free. Addy paused for a few minutes. Tapping her pencil on the floor, she thought about the ice cream parlors and streetcars. Then she continued, *But I don't know why there one freedom for colored people and one for white people. If I could ask Mr. Lincoln a question I would ask him why. Maybe now he stopped the war he can make one freedom.*

Addy wrinkled up her forehead, not sure what to write next. She sat in silence a long time without writing a word. When she heard Mrs. Golden ring the supper bell, she decided she needed to study a little more on freedom before trying again.

The next morning, Addy woke late. Poppa and Momma had gone to work. Momma had left buttermilk and cornbread for Addy to eat for breakfast. Momma also left a note on Addy's slate. She wanted Addy to go to the butcher shop and get five cents' worth of neck bones on account. Just thinking about them made Addy's mouth water. Momma added vinegar and cooked them until the meat almost fell off the bones. She was making the neck bones for church supper the next day. Their church was having a whole day of worship and song dedicated to President Lincoln.

To Addy's surprise, the butcher shop, which was normally very busy on a Saturday morning, was practically empty. There was only one woman at the counter. As she got her meat wrapped in paper, Addy noticed the woman was crying.

The butcher said, "It's a shame, I'm telling you. Lincoln was such a fine man."

Was? Addy thought.

The woman cried, "We're heading into war again."

The butcher said, "Don't go getting ahead of yourself, Mrs. Andersen."

"If they made it to Gettysburg before, they'll come marching into Philadelphia this time. There'll be cannons firing in the harbor and bullets whizzing through the streets." The woman spun around, grabbing Addy tightly by the arm. "Save yourself, child! Dig yourself a hole, and throw yourself in." Then she rushed past Addy and out the door.

Addy asked the butcher, "What happened? Did the war start again?"

"No," he said. "That Mrs. Andersen carries on so. She just thinks because the president's dead—"

Addy interrupted. "President Lincoln?" she asked in a voice stifled by fear.

"Say, haven't you heard, little girl? He was shot last night at a theater in Washington. News come in this morning. He died. The shooting was the act of a coward, I'm telling you."

Addy stepped backward, shaking her head. She didn't want to believe what the butcher was telling her.

"Hey, what did you come in for?" asked the butcher.

Addy stammered and bolted out the door, heading toward Mrs. Ford's dress shop to find Momma. Running through the streets, Addy noticed that the city looked little like it had the day before. Clusters of people gathered outside of shops. No one was smiling. The faces Addy saw started looking more and more alike. Everyone appeared to have heard the same terrible news. Addy kept running, seeing people cry openly, even grown men. Addy was crying, too. When she got to Mrs. Ford's shop, she found the door locked and the shop empty and dark.

Addy raced to the boarding house. She hadn't been this scared since she and Momma had run to freedom through the dark woods. But now Addy was running through the streets of Philadelphia in the light of day, fearing that whatever freedom she and her family had gained was about to end.

When Addy reached the boarding house, she heard grownups talking in the dining room. Before entering, Addy wiped away her tears. Mr. and Mrs. Golden, M'dear, and a boarder named Mr. Williams were there along with Momma. Addy went in and sat on Momma's lap, listening to their talk.

Mr. Williams said, "I don't see what

y'all fussing and carrying on about. Lincoln never cared nothing about us colored folks."

"That's not true. He freed the slaves," Mrs. Golden said.

Mr. Williams waved his hand and said, "I freed myself."

"Now, now," Mr. Golden added. "Lincoln was a good man. Give him that. He didn't have to open his mouth about slavery. He was shot because he was for us coloreds."

"That's right," M'dear said. "Some white people think he done too much for us."

Addy asked, "Is the war going to start again?"

Momma rubbed Addy's back and said, "The war's over, so don't go worrying."

"That poor Mrs. Lincoln," said Mrs. Golden. "Losing her husband like that."

Addy blurted out, "But what if the war ain't over? President Lincoln was the one who got everybody to stop fighting. Who going to stop it now?"

"Addy," Momma said, "there ain't no more war. Now, I can tell this grown-folk talk is troubling you. Go on up and I'll be up in a bit and bring you a cup of tea."

Addy got up, and as she left the dining room, she heard M'dear say, "Lord knows the Lincoln children woke up to nightmare this morning."

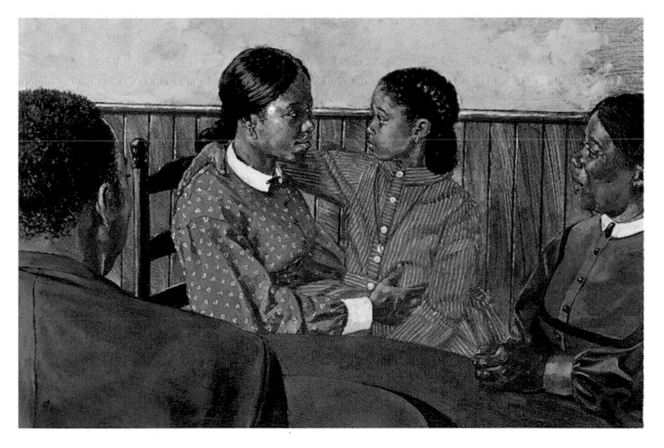

"We all have," said Momma.

Upstairs, Addy plopped down in a chair. What the adults were saying wasn't just "grown-folk talk." Addy thought, *What if the war start again? What's going to happen to Sam, to Esther?* She pinched the back of her hand. If this was all a nightmare, then maybe she could wake up and everything would be okay. But the sharp pinch didn't change anything.

There was no celebration at church the next day. Everyone sang a few songs, and then Reverend Drake started his sermon. Addy sat close to Momma in the women's section, listening.

The reverend's words flowed like clear water. "President Lincoln led us to the Promised Land. You know, Moses led his people to the Promised Land and *never* entered it. God showed it to him," Reverend Drake said, spreading his arms out. "But Moses died before he could cross

over. And our president, God rest his soul, did too."

Addy heard some of the women around her crying. Momma had her head bowed, her hands clenched in prayer.

Reverend Drake continued, "Many of you are wondering why our president was killed. And I'm here to tell you, people, I don't know. But no matter what man intends for evil, God can use for good! God is with us in all seasons, in joy and in tears. Fear not this season, for it is written in Ecclesiastes that there is 'a time to weep, and a time to laugh; a time to mourn, and a time to dance. A time to love, and a time to hate; a time of war, and a time of peace.'"

All of Philadelphia had entered its season of mourning. Addy had the week off from school, so she walked with Momma to work. A quiet clung to the city like fog. Black swags of cloth were draped over doors of shops and homes. At Mrs. Ford's dress shop, a picture of President Lincoln hung in the window. The shop was full of ladies who wanted black ruffles sewn onto their mourning dresses and cloaks. Everyone was preparing for the weekend, when President Lincoln's funeral train would arrive. There would be a procession on Saturday and a viewing of the president's body at the State House on Sunday.

On Saturday afternoon, Addy and her parents dressed in their best clothes and went to watch the procession. Poppa had picked out a spot for them on the roof of a building he had been working on for Mr. Roberts, the carpenter who had hired him just the week before. It was good they were on the roof, because it would have been hard to see anything from down below. People were lined up five deep on each side of the street. From up high, the split crowd reminded Addy of the Red Sea, parting to let Moses and his people pass through on their way to the Promised Land.

The cannon fire and gunshots made Addy jump. Poppa gave her hand a reassuring squeeze. "They saluting the president," he said.

After waiting for hours for the procession, Addy was cold and stiff, tired and hungry. It was nearly dark when eight beautiful black horses adorned with silver harnesses came into view. Their bobbing heads were topped with plumes of feathers. Behind them, the driver in his top hat sat high in a tall wagon. Addy had never seen such a fancy wagon. Its flatbed was skirted in black cloth, and the skirt was decorated with silver fringes and tassels. Black drapery hung like crescent moons along the sides. Atop the wagon was a huge black canopy. A whole story tall, it had white stripes and was topped with black plumes that looked like huge black birds. Under the canopy was President Lincoln's coffin, a long black box trimmed in silver. Momma cried as the wagon passed, and Poppa put his arm around her shoulders.

"I saw Mr. Lincoln," Mr. Roberts said, "when he was here on the way to his inauguration four years ago. He came right to the State House." He pointed up the street. "That's when he gave his speech saying he'd rather be assassinated on the spot than give up the principles of the Declaration of

Independence to save the country. He stayed true to that vow till the day he died."

When Addy had first come to Philadelphia, Miss Dunn taught the class the principles of the Declaration of Independence. She taught that all people were created equal and had rights that God had given them that shouldn't be taken away: life, liberty, and the pursuit of happiness. Those words held meaning for Addy even when she couldn't read them. She had *lived* those words during her flight to freedom. Addy thought, *President Lincoln was gonna make one freedom for everybody, just like the Declaration say. But now he can't.* Addy fought back tears as she watched the procession move out of sight.

At five o'clock the next morning, Addy and Poppa left for the State House. Momma had caught a cold and didn't feel up to going. Addy was glad to be going. She never had the chance to say hello to President Lincoln. She wanted to be able to at least say good-bye.

Just a block from the boarding house, long lines had already formed. Addy and Poppa had to snake their way back through them to get to the end, nearly two miles away. By the time the sun rose, the lines had steadily increased and didn't appear to be moving at all. When they started moving, they crept along. It took Addy and Poppa two hours to move just one block.

If yesterday the people had been a calm sea, this morning they were a restless one. There was pushing and shoving. It was cool out but hot in the lines, and Addy was glad she was with Poppa. From time to time, he hoisted her to his shoulders so Addy could take a sip of air, refreshing as a cool drink of water.

By noon, the lines had moved about half a mile. News spread down the lines that things were moving slowly because there were lines on other streets, too, all leading to the State House. Some people said they were three miles long, some said five, and they were ten people wide.

"Let me out!" a woman's voice called. "I've had enough."

Addy grabbed Poppa's hand because the pushing and shoving were getting stronger. Addy didn't know if it was the woman trying to get out or someone trying to get in, because she heard a man yelling, "Oh, no, you not butting in. I been out here since six! Go to the back of the line, or I'll crack you in the head!"

"My purse! Someone has stolen my purse. Police! Police!" another woman screeched.

Just then the crowd surged forward,

a powerful wave that ripped Addy's hand from Poppa's. People were trying to push their way out of the line, but nobody was moving to let them out. Addy yelled for Poppa, but she was being pushed deeper into the crowd. The air around her was hot. She couldn't see or hear Poppa in the crush of bodies. She felt dizzy, as if she was going to pass out.

Then she felt herself being lifted up from behind. A rush of air came over her as she was set safely on the street. Addy turned around to see who had come to her rescue. It was a white man who looked to be about Poppa's age.

"Stand back and give the child

some air," a black woman in a velvet coat said. "Honey, who are you with? Where are your people?"

Addy answered, "I'm with my Poppa." Just then she saw Poppa pushing through the crowd, and she jumped into his arms.

One of the soldiers warned the crowd, "It's enough that we've had to roust pickpocketing hooligans all day. If you cause trouble, we'll send you to the back of the lines!"

"All we want to do is pay our respects," said the white man who had rescued Addy.

"Everybody is going to have a chance," the soldier said. "Back in line!"

As Addy and Poppa made their way back into line, Addy held tightly to Poppa's hand. He turned and thanked her rescuer. "I'm grateful," Poppa said.

"It was nothing," the man said.

"It was kind," replied Poppa.

The man said, "This is a day you'll remember for the rest of your life, young lady. Don't you think so, sir?"

Addy looked at Poppa. He seemed puzzled, but then he beamed a smile that lit up his face. Never, ever had Addy heard a white man call her father "sir."

"Well, yes it is, sir. This is truly a day to remember," said Poppa.

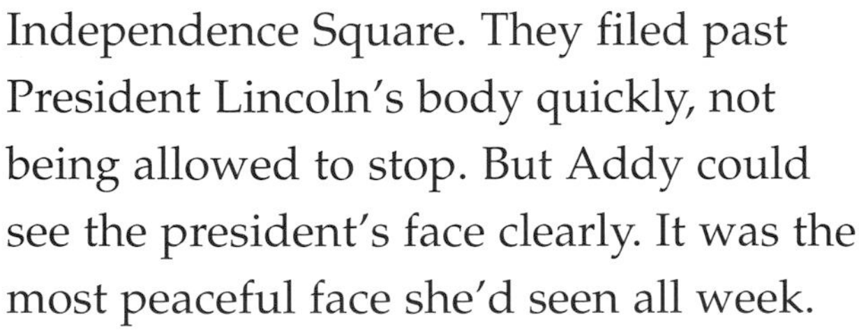

It was close to supper time when Addy and Poppa reached the State House. Like everyone else, they entered through the tall windows on Chestnut Street and exited through those at Independence Square. They filed past President Lincoln's body quickly, not being allowed to stop. But Addy could see the president's face clearly. It was the most peaceful face she'd seen all week.

As she and Poppa walked out into the dark and quiet street lit with gas lamps, Poppa said softly, "Look like the president done found peace."

"But Poppa," said Addy, "it's like the reverend say. The president like Moses.

They filed past President Lincoln's body quickly, not being allowed to stop.

He ain't make it to the Promised Land. And this ain't really no Promised Land. We ain't got freedom like white folks."

Poppa fell silent for a bit before he spoke. "Freedom don't come all at once, Addy. President Lincoln done led the way. We all the one got to follow."

Addy walked along with Poppa, listening to their footsteps echo in the night. She thought about the sea of people she'd seen from the rooftop. Black and white, those people had all come out to mourn President Lincoln's passing. She thought about Mrs. Ford and Mr. Roberts, both white people who'd given her parents jobs. And then there was that white man who had saved her from the angry sea of people today. He had showed Poppa more respect than any white man ever had.

At least some people heading in the right direction, Addy thought as she held tight to Poppa's hand and kept on walking.

CONNIE PORTER

At 11 Now

I was four when President Kennedy was assassinated. I saw his death upset my parents the way Addy saw the news of President Lincoln's death upset adults. Unlike Addy, I was too young to understand much, but I knew something bad had happened. "Grown-folk talk" had entered my world of dolls and afternoon naps, and I was grateful for the safety of my mother's lap.

Connie Porter is the author of the Addy books in The American Girls Collection.

A Peek Into the Past

THE DEATH OF LINCOLN

Lincoln presenting the Emancipation Proclamation

In the four years that Abraham Lincoln served as president of the United States, he worked hard to end slavery and to reunite a country torn apart by slavery. President Lincoln declared war on the southern states that had broken away from the Union. He also issued the Emancipation Proclamation, which said that all slaves in the South were free.

When the North defeated the South on April 9, 1865, President Lincoln was a hero to freed slaves and *abolitionists,* people who opposed slavery. But he had enemies, too. John Wilkes Booth, an actor and southern sympathizer, feared that Lincoln would give blacks too much freedom. When Booth heard Lincoln say that blacks should have the right to vote, Booth threatened to kill him.

A few days later, on April 14, Booth carried out his threat. While Lincoln and his wife were watching a play at Ford's Theatre, Booth came up behind Lincoln and shot

Booth's gun

Lincoln was watching the play ***Our American Cousin.***

him. Lincoln survived through the night but died early the next morning. The nation, which just a few days earlier had celebrated the end of the war and slavery, fell into deep mourning. One citizen said, "It seemed as if the whole world had lost a dear, personal friend."

Lincoln's funeral was held in the White House four days later, on April 19.

All across the nation, Americans crowded into churches to mourn their lost president. Many Americans had another chance to say good-bye as Lincoln's casket was carried by train toward his home in Springfield, Illinois. The funeral train traveled along the same route that Lincoln had taken

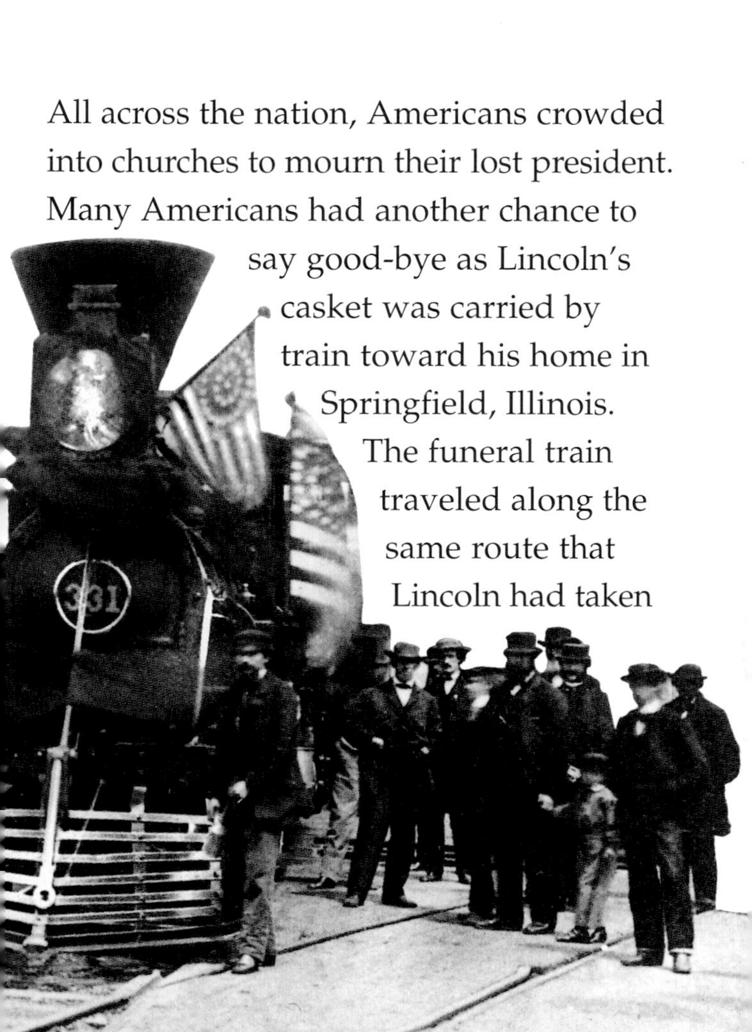

to Washington when he had been elected president four years earlier. At every stop along the way, people gathered to kneel, weep, and pay their respects.

Large cities along the route held elaborate funeral processions to honor the president. One of the grandest took place in Philadelphia on Saturday, April 22.

Lincoln's casket was placed in an ornate hearse pulled by eight black horses with silver harnesses. The procession wound its way through downtown Philadelphia, past buildings draped in black cloth and banners, toward Independence Hall. Bands played solemn music, and every 60 seconds, "minute guns" fired.

As many as half a million people—equal to the population of the entire city—gathered to watch the procession. Rivers of people lined the streets to get a close-up view of Lincoln's casket. Others, like Addy's family, watched from

The procession through downtown Philadelphia

windows, balconies, rooftops, and even treetops high above the streets.

Visitors with special invitations viewed the president's body in Independence Hall that evening, but most people had to wait until the next morning. Hundreds of people poured into the city hoping to see the president's body. Hotels overflowed, leaving many visitors to camp in the streets overnight. When Independence Hall opened at 6:00 on Sunday morning, thousands of people filled the streets. By 10:00 A.M., the lines of people were three miles long.

Lincoln's body lay in the room where the Declaration of Independence had been signed nearly 100 years before. All day and all night, people passed through the candle-lit chamber. Because thousands of people still waited outside, viewers were not allowed to stop beside Lincoln's open coffin. They strained to touch or even kiss the president as they were pushed onward.

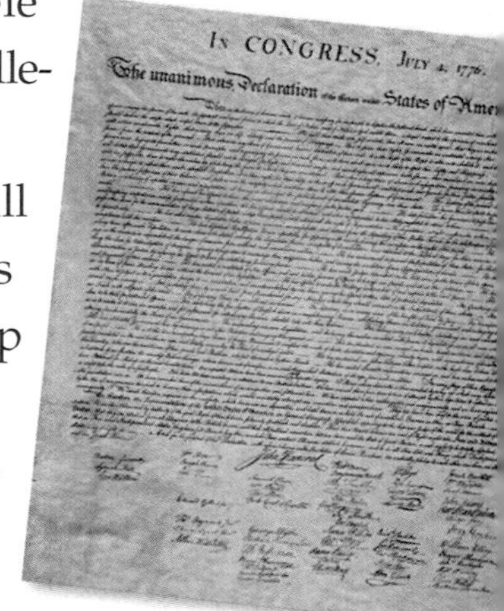
IN CONGRESS, JULY 4, 1776.

The unanimous Declaration

The Declaration of Independence

Those waiting outside were anxious and exhausted. Many had walked for miles, because it was Sunday and no streetcars were running. During the wait, chaos broke out. Some people tried to leave the lines while others pushed to get in. Clothing was torn, women fainted, and children were nearly lost underfoot. Several people were seriously injured. Still, people pressed on to see their president. By the time the funeral train left town the next morning, 300,000 people had said good-bye to Lincoln.

With Lincoln's death, many

Soldiers were stationed to help control the crowd.

Americans feared that war would break out again and that slaves would lose their freedom. But instead, people banded together to mourn and show respect for Lincoln and his beliefs. This coming together of people—black and white—gave Americans hope that the nation was strong and that Lincoln's values would not die with him. He had led his people to the "Promised Land," and they would march on.

A NATION MOURNS
The Departed
PATRIOT,
STATESMAN,
And MARTYR.

Born February 12th, 1809.
Died April 15th, 1865.

Mourning badges and banners appeared all over the country.

AN AMERICAN GIRLS PASTIME
Abraham Lincoln
Address delivered at the dedication of the Cemetery at Gettysburg.
Four score and seven years ago our fathers brought forth on this

Learn About Lincoln

Take this presidential quiz!

During Addy's time, Americans didn't know very much about President Lincoln's early years. After his death, however, many biographies were written that helped people learn more about his fascinating life.

Take this quiz to learn more facts about Lincoln's childhood, his early career, and where you can still see images of him today.

Presidential Quiz

1. As a boy, Abe Lincoln attended a "blab school." How do you think it got its name?
   a. Students said their lessons out loud until they'd memorized them.
   b. Students talked too much.
   c. Everyone blabbed about everyone else's secrets.

2. Lincoln loved to read. How far do you think he'd walk just to borrow a book that he hadn't read?
   a. 5 miles
   b. 10 miles
   c. 20 miles

3. Why do you think Lincoln Logs were named after Abe Lincoln?
    a. He liked to build forts out of logs and branches.
    b. He grew up in a log cabin.
    c. He was as tall as the trees used to build log cabins.

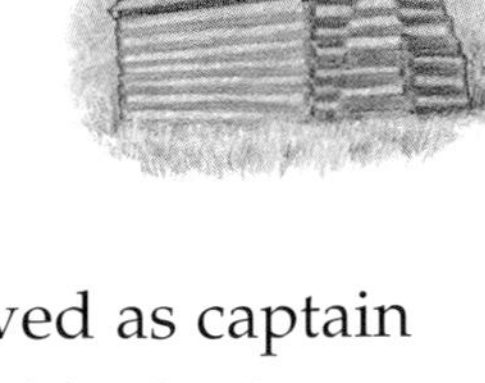

4. For 30 days, Lincoln served as captain of a militia troop. He said he had to fight only one thing. What do you think it was?
    a. soldiers
    b. poison ivy
    c. mosquitoes

5. While working as a lawyer, what do you think Lincoln kept in his tall black hat?

    a. a rabbit

    b. important papers

    c. his lunch

6. While he was president of the United States, which holiday do you think Lincoln created?

    a. Thanksgiving

    b. the Fourth of July

    c. Presidents' Day

7. Lincoln's face appears on some of the currency we use today. Where can you find him?

    a. on pennies
    b. on dollar bills
    c. on five-dollar bills

8. The statue of Lincoln at the Lincoln Memorial in Washington, D.C., stands 20 feet tall. What do you think it's made of?

    a. wood
    b. bronze
    c. marble

Answers

1. **a.** When Lincoln was in school, books and papers were scarce. Students had to learn their lessons by reciting them out loud.
2. **c.** Lincoln would walk to neighboring towns as far as 20 miles away just to borrow a book.
3. **b.** Lincoln and his family were grateful for their log cabin in Indiana. Until it was built, they lived in a shelter made of poles, brush, and leaves.
4. **c.** Lincoln's only battles were what he called "bloody struggles" with mosquitoes!

5. **b.** Lincoln kept important papers in his tall hat so that he wouldn't lose them.
6. **a.** Lincoln proclaimed the last Thursday of November 1863 as "a day of Thanksgiving and praise."
7. **a, c.** Lincoln is on both pennies and five-dollar bills.
8. **c.** The Lincoln Memorial looks like one solid piece of marble, but it's actually made of 28 blocks that fit together like puzzle pieces.

Find these books at your local bookstore or library.

Abe Lincoln: The Young Years
BY KEITH BRANDT

Back to the Day Lincoln Was Shot!
BY BEATRICE GORMLEY

The Assassination of Abraham Lincoln
BY BRENDAN JANUARY

If You Grew Up with Abraham Lincoln
BY ANN MCGOVERN

Abe Lincoln: Log Cabin to White House
BY STERLING NORTH

Abe Lincoln Grows Up
BY CARL SANDBURG